D0359975

THE STORY OF LOVIE:

Or, Establishing Ideals.

By Myrtle Fillmore
With Forward by Reverend Lei Lanni Burt

TABLE OF CONTENTS

April 9, 1991

Lei Lanni A. Burt, Minister
Unity Church of Today
P. O. Box 1042
Minden, Nevada 89423

Dear Lei Lanni,

I'm glad to be getting back to you (finally!) with answers to your questions about "The Story of Lovie" by Myrtle Fillmore. Since we spoke in January, I scanned the story and also routed it to several of my colleagues. The consensus is that the School is not interested in republishing this material, either in book or teaching format. We doubt if it would have wide enough appeal to make it a viable project for us.

However, we would certainly like to give you our blessing on publishing it yourself if you would like to do so. We would ask only that you indicate the original publishing source, as you have done in your prologue, and that you be faithful to re-copy it accurately, as you appear to have done already.. The material is not currently copyrighted, as it was published before we began this process.

I certainly wish you well in this endeavor, if it is one you choose to pursue. I am sure that God will direct you in this decision as in all others. I look forward to seeing you soon, perhaps at Conference.

Love and blessings,

Connie Fillmore

Connie Fillmore
President

CF:lt

No copyediting has been performed on the original manuscript in an effort to keep it as typed by the author.

GRATITUDES

First and foremost, I will be eternally grateful for the living loving presence of Spirit that guided my hands in the archives to the *Wee Wisdom* magazines where this story was originally published a chapter a month in the early 1900's. Second of all, my deepest gratitude to Myrtle Fillmore, co-founder of Unity, for the consciousness she lived and dared to write about.

There have been so many angels along the way who have believed in my dream to have this story published and I hesitate to name them individually so as not to neglect any one of them. From teachers, to students, to friends, and family members, each one represents an energy in the completion of this project. From my heart to yours, thank you.

Reverend Lei Lanni Burt

PROLOGUE:

*M*YRTLE FILLMORE, CO-FOUNDER OF UNITY WAS THE founder-editor of *Wee Wisdom*. The first edition was printed in August, 1893. In September of 1907, she began publishing a series story entitled "LOVIE." Her unique approach to writing and the fascinating way that she used characters to express Truth principles is a timeless treasure. The depth of Myrtle Fillmore's spiritual consciousness can be felt in an almost tangible way as one enters the world of words expressed through her. Her awareness of the healing power of prayer gave birth to the Silent Unity Prayer Ministry, and is part of the rich legacy she left for Truth seekers of all ages.

In this time, when so much of our world seems filled with uneasiness and hatred and yet more and more people across the planet are recognizing the necessity for Prayer and Truth, it seems fitting that this story becomes a printed reality.

What a thrill it is to step into the consciousness of a belief system that saw, and called forth as Jesus Christ did, the wholeness of Omnipresent Spirit. Myrtle Fillmore had a unique way of personifying Truth principles through the characters of her story. Some might even say the setting and characters aren't real enough, that they are too good to relate to life. My proposal to you, dear reader, is that perhaps this story has come forth just now in the age of technological phenomena to remind us of what living Reality could be like.

So pull up a chair, make yourself comfortable, and allow the consciousness of Myrtle Fillmore's belief to be freed in you as you enter the world of "LOVIE."

Reverend Lei Lanni Burt

INTRODUCTION

(THE AUTHOR OF THIS LITTLE STORY WISHES TO EXPLAIN TO the older readers of <u>Wee Wisdom</u> that its object is to keep before them a wholesome working out of Divine ideals, and so to stimulate and encourage in everyone the desire to bring forth life's best and highest possibilities.

So many questions are being asked and so much seeking for help in the application of these higher truths to personal problems that it has seemed to the author as though these questions could be more successfully answered and this help more efficiently given through the creation of characters that shall work out in detail the problems that stand between the race and its demonstration of dominion.

"Every seed bringeth forth after its kind." To insure the highest and best in our lives and those of our children, it is absolutely necessary that we not only perceive exalted ideals of life, but that we shall work out their exquisite patterns in the loom of our every-day living.

This is what the characters are expected to do in "The Story of Lovie," and if in working them out the reader should have to accompany our heroine through some of the most sacred and delicate experiences of life, it must be remembered that it all belongs to the full, rounded-out problem of human existence.

There has been special request that *Trixey should have a place in the new story, and so, as she has grown to young womanhood along with a goodly number of others who were once "Wees," she has been given a high trust to fulfill in expression of ideal womanhood.)

*See "Wee Wisdom's Way."

CHAPTER I.
THE CHOSEN SPOT

*O*NCE UPON A TIME THERE WAS A LITTLE SPOT OF WILDWOOD so near the heart of a great city -- you would have wondered how it could hold against the push and power of man's avarice. Fabulous sums were offered for this bit of paradise, for it was coveted by the speculator and in demand for palatial homes. Yet there it nestled like a trusting child that knows only the protection of parental love. The birds sang and the squirrels frisked, and all the denizens of that miniature forest were as free and happy as though in the depths of a country wood. It was like an oasis in the desert to the weary passers-by. There the children and all who wanted a respite from the unnatural and over-crowded life of the city, found a welcome under its green tent of trees, and Nature took them to her wholesome heart and made them forget all but the exquisite joy of living.

The little street urchins had a name of their own for this wonderful spot and it was never in the heart of any one to harm or molest one of its happy creatures. One day Pinkey and Pigeontoe, two little gamins, were steeping their benighted souls in its beauty and quiet and rolling their little rag-ga-dy bodies over the delicious grass, when Pinkey's over-flowing heart gave rise to these sentiments:

"Believe me, Kid, yer comes in here to find out what yer like; 'taint no put up job on yer here; it's all fair and honest and it makes sumpin' in yer feel different and yer'd like to get next to it."

When Pigeontoe ventured an opinion that it might be God, Pinkey's snub nose went higher up into the air and pulling himself onto his feet he assumed the lofty manner of one who knows all about it and pointing to a tall church spire visible through the foliage, he scornfully turned down Pigeontoe's philosophy with:

"Yer off yer hinges, Kid, ye'll find God in them stone piles yonder, he's too upty for a place like this and fellers like us. You've got to have glad rags and nifty manners to stand in with God. This yere is wot yer call Natur'. Natur' hain't got no cinch on nuthin'. Yer don't have to take in yer layout and rag line for her; she takes yer on tick and divies up with yer and makes yer feel like a lord. Jim told me there was a lot of it out in the country, and" ~ but Pinkey's oratory was suddenly cut short by a punch in the ribs from Pigeontoe, a signal for silence. Two gentleman had entered the ground and were coming that way.

"Some of them Wall street fellers," was Pinkey's swift comment. "Skidoo, Kid" ~ and Pinkey and Pigeontoe vanished like a flash.

The two men halted under the big oak and the creatures that had listened to Pinkey and Pigeontoe heard this conversation:

"I say, Jennings, what does Wiseman mean by giving in to the silly whim of a foolish boy and holding onto this brush patch where property is invaluable?"

"I don't know," answered Jennings, "without it is because it belongs to the boy through his mother's dowry. But, say, as long as we've struck such a nice cool spot, let's enjoy it awhile; there's no rush."

Coming under the charmed spell of the place, the other, whose name was Bond, offered no objection, and so these two Wall street princes, divested of coat and hat, stretched themselves out upon the fragrant sward. A season of delicious quiet followed, which penetrated their sordid souls and awoke blissful memories. It was Bond who broke the silence.

"I say, Jennings, this is the whole thing. By Jupiter! It makes me feel like I was back in the old woods at home. What is life now compared with those halcyon days of boyhood. I believe I'd give my millions to have them back."

"Maybe," responded Jennings, "that's what young Wiseman foresees and so intends to hold onto his boyhood and let the millions go. Not so bad an idea, eh? Bond."

"Well, if holding on to a spot like this insures perpetual youth the nature of my covetousness for the place changes and I would possess it as it is."

"That may not be impossible," answered the accommodating Jennings. "The coming marriage of young Wiseman is announced and it may make a difference in his notion about keeping this property, for I am told it is about all he inherits, and you know a wife is expensive."

"Have you ever seen this young fellow?" asked Bond, with some show of interest.

"Yes quite a number of times, he's a fine specimen of young manhood; someway, this very spot reminds me of him, he's so unlike the young men of the day."

"Well, I hope he'll stay so," blurted Bond. "It's as rare a thing to find a young man of that sort these days as it is to run across a spot like this. They belong together."

Jennings reserved his opinion and silence followed. The birds looking down saw two men wrapped in blissful dreams and trilled soft and low lest they should waken them.

After a long, long time a busy bee buzzing too near the ear of Mr. Bond shattered his drowsy dreams through its suggestion of activity and brought him back to the world of affairs. Consulting his gold repeater he called out to Jennings that they'd wasted a whole hour in that fool place and he'd be blanked if he didn't believe it was charmed. Jennings arose, shook himself and laughingly declared they had been under the wholesome charm of Nature for one whole hour. Re-clothing themselves with coat and hat, these two princes of the world hastily left the spot without even a regretful glance backward. A thrill of sound followed their exit like the titter of suppressed mirth, and then all its creature-fold gathered themselves in and about the big oak to discuss the late visitors.

"Just to think," laughed Robin, "of their coming under the charm."

"But the queerest thing," chattered the squirrel, "was calling a little rest and happiness, waste of time." And so these happy creatures brought to naught the wisdom and gold of Wall street. Only mourning dove seemed cast down and concerned, and as last inquired:

"Do you really think this marriage will make a difference?"

"Why, you foolish dove," giggled the robin, "where were your ears last evening when he said right under this very tree to her, 'Of all the places in the world this is the one for you and me.'"

"And didn't she put her sweet arms as far around me as they would go," said the oak and whisper to me that some day she was going to live with us? Difference? Well I should rustle, it would make a difference her being with us always."

Then followed a long discussion which went unrecorded, but which made you wonder who this wonderful "he" and "she" might be to whom this little kingdom offered such loving allegiance.

When the wood grew full of long shadows all the creature-folk were back at the big oak again, and you were certain of a great expectance, for you could have heard like a wave of melody the conscious rustle of the spreading branches and the soft pipings of hundreds of little throats, then suddenly all was silent for there stood beneath the big oak a youth and maiden, and you beheld in them the king and queen of this enchanted forest.

Chapter II.
THE LOVERS

*T*HE LISTENING BIRDS HEARD THE "OLD STORY" OVER AGAIN, but not after the old manner for these young lovers possessed a love that not only enriched and ennobled their own lives, but radiating out, spread joy and warmth to all about them. He was saying to her:

"Do you know, Trixey, this is sacred ground to me? I stood upon this very spot once, when I was so young that my memory holds nothing of that time save this one indelible picture. My mother stood beside me, as you do now. There were soft white clouds floating in the sky, and as I stood gazing up through the branches of this giant oak it seemed as if it reached and reached until it touched the far-away sky, and I wondered could I climb up there, would I be among the clouds and stars and angels? I told my happy fancies to my mother. I shall never forget her glorious smile as she drew me close to her heart and told me there were greater heights for her dear boy to climb. And then she put into my hand an acorn that had fallen and explained to me how this great tree had once seemed a helpless little mite like that, but in its heart had held the germ of this mighty promise it has now fulfilled. Then she broke the shell of the little acorn and showed me how tiny was the image of the oak tree slumbering there, and how like that acorn there slumbered in me the image and likeness of a divine **possibility** which I should bring forth some day to tower among mankind even as this giant oak towers among its comrades. I was to be great and good and noble and mighty. A great thrill of joy swept through my being and something awoke within my little heart that made it feel strong and able to bring forth this mighty manhood, and again my mother clasped me to her and breathed a prayer, so sweet and strong, it seemed to wrap me about in soft white folds of peace. And then I promised her I would be all the waiting image called for.

"But oh, the days that came and went after the inspiration of her presence was removed from me. Only he who watches with us ever could know the struggles of my wretched little heart. I was left alone to the care of tutors and servants, for my father was too much engrossed in finances to spare me time and then how could he understand about the divine image in me that struggled for expression, any more than he had understood the spiritual nature of my mother?

"I found consolation in retreating to this blessed spot. My father never denied me this; perhaps he felt it was a tie between me and **her**. This little woodland was my mother's gift to me, and I have never spoken it aloud before, but it is as if every tree and shrub and creature here were mother's messengers to remind me. It may be a fancy born of  my great love for her, but some way, she is always an invisible presence to me here." He paused for a moment, for his voice had sunken into an inaudible whisper. "Some way, Trixey, some way, I feel the intervening veil between the 'here-and-there,' is so thin at this spot that mother can look through and see and know all about us now. I have little beside my love and this Eden to offer you, but have we not learned, that 'life is more than meat and the body more than raiment,' and is not the union of our rich young souls more than all the world beside can give?" A gentle pressure on his hand first spoke for her. And then, turning her sweet face up to him she said:

"Dear Jack, you give me more than all the world beside and I in turn, endow you with my maiden heart and all the riches of the Omnipresent Good."

He bent and kissed her upturned face, saying:

"Trixey, the world of lovers could not understand why, dear as we have been to each other, I had never asked a kiss of you before.

"But you appreciate that I have waited till this holy moment for this sacrament of our love. I hold that a kiss is holy and whoso kisses lightly knows nothing of the sacredness of love. My mother's kiss and yours are all my lips have known. All that I am, all that I hope to be, I owe to the ideals you and she have held for me. Could mothers and maidens but know this power to save from the 'snare of the fowler' the feet of their sons and lovers, there would be more happy ones like us, Trixey."

Again the sweet voice which you both felt and heard rippled on the soft air.

"Dear Jack, it had never occurred to me that kissing had any part in our comradeship, and I do thank you for making it a sacred and not a common part of our love."

His smile was broad and genial as he answered, "Yes, little girl, we will always be comrades, you and I. But since we are to become citizens of these sweet wilds we must be hunting up a place to pitch our tent."

Then followed the most delightful season of exploration. Every tree in the little wood felt the touch of caressing hands and

every blade of grass the pressure of loving feet. The creature-fold frisked and winged about to keep up with the explorers. And there was great glee over the antics and apparent curiosity manifested by these little neighbors.

I believe," said Trixey, sending forth one of her rollicking laughs, "that we had better consult our future neighbors before we decide on settling here; they may consider us intruders. They have the first right."

"Oh you don't understand them like I do, I have been so much among them. I flatter myself it is rather an ovation than a protest they are giving us. They will be glad to have us here. I feel it in their friendly chatter. We will not infringe upon their rights. They will be cheerful and considerate little neighbors."

When the site for the bungalow was chosen several big trees stood in the way, but Trixey planned that they should still have their part in the home-making, for their big trunks and limbs could be used in helping to make this little bungalow harmonious with its surroundings. "A little cabin-like thing," Trixey said.

"We will have the artisians come after the birds have gone South, and when it will least interfere with those who enjoy these haunts. I wonder, Trixey, what you will think of the motley crew that find rest and pleasure here. It has been one of the greatest joys of my life that I could contribute something toward giving these products of an unwholesome civilization a little taste for freedom and Nature. I wonder, Trixey, if you will mind leaving the grounds open to them after we are settled here?"

You should have seen her face as she turned in answer, surely the light that shone upon it had not sifted through those heavy shadows.

"Dear Jack," she said, "do you not know me yet that you should question my love for the 'least of these, my brethren?' Not only can they have their old privileges, but we will see what we can do toward broadening and bettering these crippled lives. Why, Jack, we'll start a new civilization right here in our own little kingdom, and we'll lead these souls into the light and truth of a new glad life."

And as he took her to his heart he said, "God gave the best of himself when be bestowed upon mankind pure and noble womanhood."

Chapter III.
THE HOME NEST

*T*HE LITTLE FOREST HAD TWICE CHANGED ITS COLORINGS since the happenings last recorded and was putting on the soft-greens of early Spring. The magic kiss of the Spring sunshine had waked the violets and Spring beauties and loosed the pulses of glad life throughout the little wood. Birds were singing, insects humming, plant and creature alike were rejoicing in the munificence of Spring. It was the robin who stayed at home that called the attention of the returning birds to the little home-nest builded in their absence. And the chorus of praise grew louder and sweeter  because of the great love and joy this little home provided for. And it seemed as if the violets and Spring beauties grew brighter when they looked up and found this new child of the woods in their midst; for there, like a very part of the woods itself, stood "the-little-cabin-like-thing," Trixey and Jack had planned that happy Summer afternoon.

Into the midst of this Spring joy sauntered two gentlemen evidently too much engrossed in conversation to notice this new marvel till they had run upon it.

"By jove!" exclaimed a familiar voice, "what have we here, Jennings?"

"I should think," replied the astonished Jennings, "the wood-nymphs have builded a home. Did you ever see anything so elegantly harmonious with surroundings? This is what I call high art. I'd like to know the architect."

At this point the door of the bungalow opened, and a bright young fellow stepped out upon the veranda, seeing the strangers he smiled and remarked upon the beauty of the day. Jennings answered, "I trust we are not trespassing, but once having found this enchanting spot we wanted another glimpse of it. We were not aware that it was inhabited, nor were we prepared for a thing like this."

"You cannot trespass here, this is one place in the big city that is free to all who enjoy it, and this little home-nest is built here in the trees for Jack Wiseman and his bride who are soon to return from abroad. He is very fond of this spot and loves every creature of these woods," was the young man's reply.

Bond and Jennings exchanged glances, and Jennings ventured to say, "Jack Wiseman is a fine fellow and surely there could never be a more unique nest for a pair of doves to coo in than this. I am much impressed with the originality and art displayed in its construction. Could you kindly favor us with the address of the architect?"

The young man looked down and a deep blush crept over his fair face, but there was a twinkle of humor in his eyes as he made answer:

"It was the fancy of the bride herself, that the trees which were sacrificed for this building spot, having grown here, rightly belonged here and so must be woven some way, into the warp and woof of her home, and you behold the result."

"But," insisted Jennings, "it took somebody with artistic genius to work out her fancies and produce results like this."

"Oh, yes," quickly answered the young man, "her brother is an architect and of course it was such a pleasure for him to embody his sister's ideal of a home, that he may have excelled himself." Bond smiled shrewdly at the young man as he said:

"We need look no farther for the architect ~ all we lack now is the name."

"As you will," replied the young man with a hearty laugh, that shook off all his embarrassment: "Here is his card."

I read:

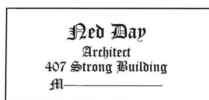

Ned Day
Architect
407 Strong Building
M————————

Bond was evidently getting interested in this young fellow and lingered, even after Jennings admonished him that time for some engagement was at hand.

"I will see you again," was his word at parting, and I hope to know your sister and young Wiseman. I have long known his father." Bond afterward confessed to Jennings, "I can't tell what it is about that young fellow, but I'd trust him with all I have."

Jennings smiled, for he inwardly knew that the ingenuousness of the boy had punctured the soul of the sordid millionaire. As Ned stood looking after the retreating pair, he remembered they had not given him their names, but he knew from their general make-up they were wealthy men of the world. His meditations were cut short by a voice within the bungalow, and as he answered, "All right, Tom: what is it?" a muscular young fellow with a good face and pleasant voice made his appearance.

"I've finished putting down the rugs," he explained, "and I was a thinkin' how Miss Trixey was always likin' runnin' water and what's to hinder puttin' a little brook down there among the unevenness in the south corner, with water cress and ferns growin' along it?"

"It's a very pretty idea, Tom, but you know that those artificial streams mean lots of money and work, and Jack is mostly dependent upon his own efforts since this place represents his fortune."

"But," argued Tom, "the old man's awful rich, ain't he, and what's hurtin' to strike him for the money?"

"That would never do Tom. Mr. Wiseman is very unapproachable, and then, too, Jack would never consent to ask a favor of anybody; he's very proud to earn his own livelihood and pay his own bills, and we could not offer him greater insult than to apply to his father."

"That's good stuff," said Tom admiringly, "but I wish I had the money. Miss Trixey should have the little runnin' water and no one would be the wiser. I never could do enough for her and you. You were the making of Tom Sams. Why! don't I remember how Tom Sams' name stood for all kinds of deviltry and meanness? nobody believed in Tom Sams till you got hold o' him ~ never will the day grow dim, when you spoke them first kind words to me, and I a mockin' at your crutch, too. Oh, Mr. Ned, them are the kind o' things that count, and never will the angels in heaven get tired o' tellin' what good's come of it." Here Tom's reminiscence was interrupted by the "chug chug" of an Auto and the arrival of a stately old gentleman whom Ned addressed as Mr. Wiseman.

"I've run up to see if things were ready. Jack has wired that they will be here in the course of a week and"~ sweeping the little bungalow with his haughty glance, he continued, "I suppose no persuasion will alter Jack's determination to take immediate possession of this little hut."

It took a moment of strenuous silence to enable Ned to quell the tumult of resentful thought that followed such ungracious reference to the pretty home, but remembering, "He maketh his sun to shine on the just and on the unjust," the sting was gone, and Ned invited the haughty father in to inspect preparations for himself. A few minutes later he was standing before a portrait which hung on the walls of the beautiful living room; oblivious to all else, he was gazing with longing eyes upon it.

It was the face of a woman in the prime of womanhood. A strong, pure sweet face, that lacked only joy to make it radiantly beautiful. As he looked something stirred beneath the crust of his haughty exterior and like a pain that had no remedy it worked at his heart. The past arose before him. He saw and felt and knew as never before what had been lacking in the life of this glorious woman. Why these perfect lips should be a trifle too firm and this sweet smile but half formed while the eyes bore the unmistakable shadow of patient sorrow. Who can describe the agony of a soul crusted over with selfishness, when remorse thrusts its keen blade through into the quick of the living consciousness.

The figure before the portrait quivered with the intensity of such experience and with a swift glance about to see if anyone were present he fell upon his knees before it and wept.

The man who came forth a half an hour later bore the evidence of one who had been overtaken "on his way to Damascus," and smitten down before the vision of a sacrificed life. Though his manner was that of one trying hard to assume the old proud authority, yet his form was bent and his voice broken when he joined the young architect on the veranda and proposed the addition of a rustic garage to the little home in the woods.

"For," he explained, "since this is my son's choice. I desire that nothing be left undone that may secure comfort or beauty here." A new tenderness crept into his voice as he proceeded:

"This little wood was his mother's gift to Jack. She was very fond of coming here and Jack is so like her he would never part with it though millions have be offered him. I have thought him foolish and withheld from him, hoping to force him to sell it, but I now see the boy was wiser than I. I want his life to be what mine is not ~ a happy, unselfish one."

Ned was silent, for it seemed a time when only silent comfort could be applied and in his heart he felt and knew some great change had been wrought through the influence of that portrait. At this juncture Tom appeared on the scene and asked for further instructions. The young architect introduced him as the chief artisan of the work just completed, and recommended him to Mr. Wiseman as the one to consult in matters of further improvement.

Ned gave Tom a meaning smile as he handed the eager father over to him, for he knew between them the dream of the "runnin' water" would be realized.

CHAPTER IV

DAWN

*I*N THE GLOW OF THE EARLY TWILIGHT, WHILE YET "THE morning stars sang together," the feathered orchestra of the little wood was a-tune and joining in. To the slender figure standing with the bared head, facing the dawning splendor of the unrisen sun, it was as if heaven and earth were uniting in one grand symphony of welcome to the coming day. So full of the beauty and harmony of the morning was the soul of Ned Day that it burst from his lips in a song of praise:

> "Oh, blessed Light! Oh, blessed Life!
> There is no discord in thy earth or heaven;
> Thou art the endless harmony that runs through all.
> Thou art the Songster and the song,
> Thou art the Giver and the gift,
> Thou art the Love and the loved,
> Thou art the Glory and the glorified,
> Thou art the Knower and the known.
> Thou art the One in all, the all-in-one;
> Thou art, and thou art God."

The morning held something more for Ned Day than the music of the spheres and the song of birds. He was about to be called to demonstrate the harmony and oneness his soul had realized, for out of the shadows had filed three grotesque little images of humanity and planted themselves where his eyes must fall upon then when he took them from the skies. A moment later and Ned Day faced his problem. Could he, would he, reconcile these dirty little gamins with the divine beauty and harmony that were pulsating his soul? The question was quickly settled, for Ned Day no sooner beheld these little faces turned up to his than a smile of welcome broke over his countenance, and his voice took on the quality of comradeship as he called out cheerily, "Hello, fellows! You're out early." There came a chorus of "Hellos" in return, and then Pinkey, edging closer, touched Ned softly as if to make sure that he was really flesh and blood, and said, "Me an' Crutches an' Pigeontoe cummed on business, but them nifty words o' yourn landed us. They make such queerness here," and Pinkey's hand went somewhere between his heart and stomach, "And I feel I orter know somthin'!"

There was a hungry, eager look in Pinkey's face quite new to it. Something had stirred in his soul ~ the awakening thrill of a new life had swept through his being. There was no half-way with Pinkey. Conviction and action went together with him. Ned realized this and felt the importance of the task before him. The sun was just lifting a golden disc above the horizon. He called the attention of the boys to it with the question:

"What is that great ball of light coming up from the East?"

There was prompt answer, "The sun."

"Where is it coming from?"

"Dunno."

"Were you expecting it?"

"Yes."

"Why?"

"Cause it allers comes round in the mornin'."

"Why does it always come in the morning?"

It was Crutches answered the question,
"God makes it come."

"Why does God make it come, Pinkey?"

"Search me," said Pinkey.

But Crutches swung a step forward and almost whispered to Ned:

" 'Cause he loves us."

"And what do you think about it, Pigeontoe?" enquired Ned of that young worthy.

Now Pigeontoe, like many bigger folks, could reiterate somebody else's opinion better than venture one of his own, and his answer was:

"My grandmar allers 'lowed God done all them things fer folks."

"Well, now," said Ned, "we know the sun does come every morning, and never fails us, and that there could be no warmth or light without it; neither could there be any life or growth. So we are bound to believe the Power that made the sun and keeps it coming to us with the morning must mean good for us. And its name is Good, only people have shortened it to God."

Pinkey flashed down from the log he had perched on. Something new had dawned upon him, and to think was to act with him.

"Oh, Mr. Ned, haint nobody got no cinch on God then?"

"Why, no, my boy. Doesn't his sun shine on everybody alike?"

Pinkey cogitated a moment, and then answered a little sorrowfully:

"Yes, but them big sky scrapers and stone piles don't give no show here."

"Well, Pinkey, it's good to know it's shining anyway, and so it's good for our souls to feel that a great Life and Love belong to them, which outshine the sun and cannot be hidden by sky scrapers or stone walls."

"Be yer meanin' God, and war that what makes the queerness in here?" and Pinkey's hand again sought the region of his stomach.

"Yes, Pinkey, that's just what I mean. It is the everywhere Good ~ God ~ that gives us the life that dwells in our bodies, and the love that makes us kind to each other, and shines through us in good thoughts and deeds."

"But I haint good," burst in Pinkey.

"Yes he is, Mr. Ned," chimed in Crutches, "he never makes fun of anybody, and fights off the boys that bullies me and brings me up here among the birds and trees where I can have a chance. He's awful good when you know him."

"That's the Great Good shining through you, Pinkey. Be careful and don't shut it out with sky scrapers and stone piles. Just let it shine."

Pinkey was silent and full of thought. Crutches told how he loved the little woods, and how it seemed like God was a lot closer here than anywhere, 'cepting where mother was.

Through careful questioning, Ned learned that Crutches had once had a nice home, but his father had gone away to the gold fields seeking his fortune, and had not been heard from for several years. And that after living up what he had left them his mother was struggling to support herself and crippled boy by working in a factory. It was plain that Crutches was well born and had a refined and sensitive nature, as well as a bright mind, in his slender little body. When the matter of his lameness was referred to, Pinkey was on the spot ready to explain the business proposition that had brought them out so early.

"Yer see, Mr. Ned, yer helpin' man war a-telling me and Pigeontoe that he knowed you onst when you's game just like Crutches, and yer cum out o' it all one night; so me an' him toted Crutches down here to find out how you done it."

Ned took in the situation, there was only one thing to be done, his mind and heart agreed upon that; but before he could carry out his plans, these dusty, hungry little beings must be washed and fed.

Janie and Tom, the presiding geniuses of the bungalow, entered into the spirit of the occasion, and in one short hour wrought a wonderful transformation in these little urchins, turning them over to Ned again clean as a whistle, with shining faces and satisfied stomachs. It was as if they'd suddenly come upon heaven and the angels, Crutches explained afterwards.

Ned proposed to Pinkey and Pigeontoe that they leave Crutches in his care for the day, coming for him in time to be home to meet his mother.

Pinkey said, "It was a go." And so it came about that the boy listened to the story of Ned Day's healing, and carried away in his heart the germs of a living faith.

CHAPTER V.

THE HOME COMING

*C*OMING, COMING," SANG THE BIRDS. C~UMMING, c~umming," hummed the bees.

"Coming, coming," rustled in the big oak, and every leaf and flower and living creature in the little forest joined the refrain, "Coming, coming." Anyway, that's how it seemed to the little group waiting on the piazza of the bungalow, for the day and the hour had arrived for the homecoming of its king and queen.

"Just to think of Miss Trixey's bein' here in a few minutes and findin' all these surprises," was the exultant comment of Tom Sams.

"She'd never dream of me and you bein' here to look after things, either," and the rest of Janie's remarks were lost in the snowy apron she applied to her mouth to subdue the happy giggle that her thought of Miss Trixey's surprise had inspired.

"It is truly wonderful," said Ned, "how everything has worked out, not a thing planned or wished, but it has been promptly provided for, and today we are ready to turn over their little kingdom to them, in order and completeness. Even their delay of a few weeks was a part of the divine order to help you out with your plans, Tom." And so the happy conversation went on till the sound of wheels grated on the new driveway, and then a moment more, and Jack and Trixey stood in speechless admiration before "the little cabin-like thing." When Trixey found her voice, she cried:

"Oh, Ned, I never dreamed it could be so beautiful as this!"

Then followed such greetings and explanations as are sacred to the "Chosen Spot."

Within as without, surprises greeted the home-comers ~ none more gratifying to Madam Trixey than the fact that Janie Smith was installed as maid and housekeeper in her pretty new home.

"I wanted to come awfully," explained Janie later on, when they were reconnoitering the kitchen and pantries, "and so your mother let me stay with her a few months just to learn how to do things like you're always used to, and I'm here, and I hope you'll like it, for I want to pay back some of the good things you have done for me."

"Dear, dear Janie," said Trixey, putting her arms round the devoted girl, "your presence here makes me very happy, and you are a blessing to my pretty home, and will always keep me remembering that no kind act is ever lost. You and I will serve the Good together, and the motto of our home shall be "**Loving Kindness.**'"

In the sittingroom Jack had discovered his mother's portrait, and without knowing the power it exercised over his father, he too fell on his knees before it, and cried aloud, "Oh, mother, mother, could you but smile upon me!" Trixey found him here and without seeming to notice his longing gaze, she said brightly, "That is Aunt Joy's and Grace's wedding gift to you, Jack. Grace painted it herself from that sweet little portrait you loaned me of your mother. How do you like it?"

Jack turned and smiled, "Grace did that! the little minx! Who would ever have thought it, Trixey? There's a wonderful livingness about it that startles one. How could she have gotten into the secrets of mother's soul so as to have pictured them in her face like that?"

"Oh, you see, Jack, that is easily accounted for. Aunt Joy was her critic, and you know Aunt Joy and your mother were inseparable friends, and so she and Grace have managed the picture very cleverly," explained Trixey.

"I wonder if father has seen **it**," remarked Jack to Ned, who had just entered the room.

"Your father has seen it," replied Ned in a voice that permitted no further questioning.

Oh, such a delightful repast as Janie served in their dainty breakfast room, and never were there such grateful hearts as Jack's and Trixey's.

"This goes beyond my ideal of a home, Jack, as much as I have stretched my imagination, I have really never compassed so much as this. Just to think, Ned will be with us part of the time, and Janie and Tom are ours for good. I'd like to divide our happiness with the whole world, Jack."

"Dear little Trixey, Sweetheart, you'll have abundant opportunities to do that, but we will not let the world divide its imagined miseries with us."

When the happy first meal was over, Tom was on hand to chaperone them about the wood.

Once outside, Jack's eye fell upon the rustic garage, and with a long whistle, he looked askance at Ned. "It was your father's idea," answered Ned. "He said you would need a way of getting out of the woods."

"My father!" exclaimed Jack, "My father did that for me?"

"Yes, go in and see your fine machine."

"Isn't it a beauty, Jack?" was Trixey's comment, but Jack was like one stunned; he could not reconcile this with the habits characteristic of his father.

"Come on, " called out Tom, who was eager to steer the home-comers 'round to "the place of running water." With the love and greetings that had to be bestowed upon everything alike in this realm of happy creatures, it was quite a time before Tom succeeded in bringing about the **denouement** of the little stream. They came suddenly upon it as they rounded a little knoll. There it lay like a pretty infant in its bed of white sand, cuddled in among fern and water cress. Trixey shrieked her delight as she sprang down beside it. "Oh, Jack, my dream is fulfilled; it always had running water in it and ferns. Surely the wonder-workers have been busy all over these little woods. Where did it all come from, Ned?"

"Ask Tom, over there, he's the wonder-worker here," answered Ned.

"You Tom? is this your work? How did you do it?"

"Well, Miss Trixey, I s'pose you might call me the instigator of it, 'cause I had it in my heart, but it's Mr. Jack's father you can thank for it. He's the one who furnished the funds, and told me to make it just as beautiful as I could."

Again Jack exclaimed, "My father! did my father do this for us?"

"Why, of course," answered Tom, who saw no occasion for surprise. "Your father is one of the cleverest old gentlemen I ever saw. He just wanted us to do everything that could be done to make this place nice and comfortable for you and Miss Trixey."

Jack passed his hand over his forehead, as if to make sure he was awake. Could it be his dream and the apparently hopeless one of his blessed mother were coming to pass, even as Trixey's about the little running stream that flowed at their feet! He turned to Ned with the question, "Has father been here lately?"

"Yes," was Ned's answer, "and he will be here today, for he knows you are come."

Trixey said she believed she'd stay and enjoy her "sylvan retreat" awhile. Tom delightedly watched her from a distance, and felt amply repaid for his part in bringing her dream to pass.

Jack Wiseman and Ned Day walked slowly toward the bungalow. Both were silent. Jack's mind was filled with the strange emotions that had been stirred through these evidences of his father's apparent interest in his new home. What could have brought about such sudden change, and what would be his father's greeting to him?

Ned understood the situation and was silently rejoicing in the thought that Jack would find his father's true heart that had been hidden away all these years beneath the hard exterior of a sordid businessman. He felt, too, as he stood on the veranda later, that Jack had sought again the presence of his mother's picture; and as Mr. Wiseman drew up and alighted from his automobile, Ned was at his side, and pointing to the "little hut," said, "Jack is in there." That was all the father desired just then, and in a moment more father and son stood before that face looking down upon them from the wall, and a new and sacred relationship sprang up between them.

Chapter VI.

TRIXEY'S LETTER HOME

*D*EAR FATHER, MOTHER, GRACE AND AUNT JOY ~
Just to think of it! Your little Trixey is installed mistress
of the dearest home that ever blessed a woman's heart. I am
happy, oh, so happy! it seems as if one little heart could not
contain the joy I feel, and so Jack offers his big one to help
me out.

I wonder were the first couple as happy in their Eden as we in
ours. You should see ours. Our home is the most marvelous
creation you ever behold. Ned has carried into its architecture
all the **woodsey** effects of these little wilds, without interfering
at all with the elegance and comfort of a city home. I was wild
with joy when I first beheld it, and so was Jack. One surprise
after another awaited us till we were in a perpetual state of
exclamation. To find Janie Smith here installed as housekeeper,
and everything going on just like it does at home, with nothing
left unthought of! And then to think, it is **our** home ~ Jack's
and mine! Where can I find words great enough to praise the
munificent Giver! It is as if everything I had ever dreamed
of or wished for had found its way to this home of Jack's
and mine.

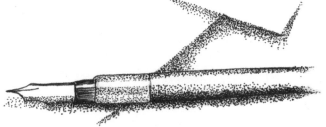

I am writing this letter in my little boudoir ~ Ned calls it "Queen Trixey's throne room," whatever he means by that. It is a dream of loveliness, and I suspect has been finished in white in remembrance of my childish love for Aunt Susan's pretty white room. The doors are cherry with tall mirrors in them, the rest of the woodwork is creamy white. And oh, the decorations are so exquisitely delicate one might fancy an angel had plucked her wings to give softness and beauty to it all. The same old feeling comes over me of the Great Brooding Whiteness that soothes and blesses, and shall at last wrap humanity about and heal it of its sorrows and pain.

Through the open window comes the song of the wood birds. Such freedom and happiness as they express! We call them our little neighbors, and Jack really believes all these wood creatures take a personal interest in us and our affairs. They have never been frightened or interfered with and so are fearless, and whenever we go about outside, we have a retinue of them in attendance, and Jack really thinks they understand everything he says to them; for you know they have been comrades all his precious life. It is really very interesting to watch them, and I am beginning to find out that in some ways they manifest more intelligence than man.

We are getting very close to Nature, and we feel that she is adopting us. I am reminded of Grace's idea about Nature being Mother-God. I believe it is a true one. Think of the wonderful motherliness which manifests in her bending skies and cradling earth, and the soft lullabys she sings through rustling trees and babbling brooks. And then her great providing breasts, nourishing alike all the children of earth regardless of race or color. Yes, Grace, darling, you were right; God is not a bachelor.

Fairy tales are without interest and color compared with our living realities. Just to think of "Wiseman's Wildwood," that is the name Jack and I have decided on for our home, having all these years eluded the clutches of the greedy world and nestled here in undisturbed naturalness, just waiting for Jack and me! **For Jack and me,** oh, my heart is so full it would seem at this moment God's completeness is ours and there is nothing more to wish. But the "bright idea still glows down upon us," and we know there is more to follow. And we also know, that the only way to keep happiness is to give it away. You will see some of these days Jack's ideals and mine reaching out until they include every living creature.

But I have not told you of the prattling young brook that has found its way into our wildwood. You remember it has always been a fancy of mine that running water and my soul had some common joy. Well, Tom Sams has contrived to gratify this fancy, and through some magic maneuver or legerdemain, has brought into visibility the dearest little stream down in the south end. It looks as if it had its source in a hidden spring under a great rock, and as it flows forth into the bed of white sand, it ripples and murmurs and nestles among the ferns and cresses, and then meanders along through little knolls and fringing bushes as naturally as if it were a born child of the woods. And I am inclined to believe its prattling presence has become not only a joy and pleasure to the wood folk, but a contribution to their necessities.

It was Jack's father who insisted upon carrying out Tom's plans for this thing of my dreams, and he really seemed as much delighted as Tom over its success.

He is so lovely to us. He comes every day to see us, and though Ned says he called our pretty home "a little hut" once, yet now I know he thinks it beautiful. There's something in the atmosphere of it he does not understand, and yet his hungry soul delights itself in it.

Jack says he is so changed, and Ned dates it from the time he first ran across that picture of Grace's. Ned says it made such a wonderful impression upon him that after he had spent half an hour with it he was not the same man.

Jack thinks it the most wonderful picture that ever was painted. He says it almost breathes, and he can hardly comprehend that it is the work of our little Grace. But we know the Great Genius waits to do the bidding of whosoever will. And our Grace is versed in the "open sesames" of mind and soul.

Although we have found no wood nymphs about the place, it seems there are gnomes and brownies a-plenty. Jack called me out a while ago to see some of them. He had three waiting. You should have seen them! Pinkey, Pigeontoe and Crutches. Pinkey comes first, that's his nature, and his name I judge is derived from the shock of red hair he uncovered in my honor. Pigeontoe, as his name indicates, toes in, and the other, Crutches, is a little cripple. Pinkey is a character, with the brightest eyes and quickest mind imaginable, but his language is something terrible. Why, I couldn't understand a thing he meant, and Jack was convulsed with laughter over it and declared I would soon get used to street parlance, but I'm sure I don't want anything of that kind, and I shall undertake teaching them English right away. Pigeontoe is more common, but his speech is a little more comprehensible; still he needs lessons in English, too. Crutches' pathetic little face goes right to my heart. He seems refined, too, and speaks correctly. Judge my surprise when he lifted his great blue eyes to mind and said, "Miss Wiseman, I'm going to be well, like Mr. Ned some day." And then the child proceeded to open his heart to me. His faith is beautiful, and he has fine ideals, and oh, I am so glad we shall be able to help him realize them. He thinks Pinkey the most wonderful boy on earth, and I'm rather interested in him myself, when he learns to talk decently. I think I'll start right in teaching them. Jack wants to know if he shall clear out the garage or build an academy for my school. I think, for the present, the shade of the big oak will answer.

Such a long letter as I have written you, and yet I have only just skimmed over what there is to tell. Can't you come, all of you, soon, and see for yourselves this wonderful paradise of Jack's and mine?

Ever with fond love, in which Jack joins me, I am your

Trixey.

CHAPTER VII

MORE IDEALS

HE DIAL OF THE YEAR HAS TURNED THRICE ROUND SINCE the coming of our king and queen. Spring has spread again her green tents in the woodland kingdom; again awakened her sleeping beauties; again recalled her feathered orchestra from the southland and set astir the pulses of glad life in all her creatures.

So much like that other spring seems this one, you would never know from anything apparent it were not the same. No change in song of bird, or hum of bee, or hue of flower, or rustling leaf. No trace of the three intervening years has record here. The seasons are God's calendar, the years, man's measure of events.

But, while yet we meditate, two boyish figures bound into sight and make a race for the big oak. "I touched it first," was the joyful shout of the winner.

"All right," cheerily called out his fellow, "those legs will fetch you every time," and unable to express their exuberance of spirit otherwise, the two boys locked in the embrace of a wrestle and rolled on the soft sward. There's something strangely familiar about these two boys, that bright poll bobbing up and down on the grass strongly resembles Pinkey's, and those big blue eyes are very like Crutches, but then these boys are clean

and well dressed and would raise their hats and speak to you in good English, you are quite sure of that; then, too, they are both strong and well, and there is no sign of crutches.

As if to answer our puzzle, the bright-haired boy leaves off with his romping and setting himself up against the big oak calls out ~

"I say, Crutches," then recalling himself he jumps to his feet and bumps his head three times against the oak tree, with the self-admonition, "now I guess you'll remember," then turning to his blue-eyed companion he explained, "I didn't go to do it, for I promised Miss Wiseman I never would call you that old name again, and I'll bump harder than that if I ever do, but, I'll never forget again, you see if I do! She told me the story of King Richard so's to help me remember, always, 'Richard is himself again.'"

"Oh you're all right, Phillip," replied blue eyes, "a little slip like that's nothing. I'm strong and well, and if the boys should call me that I wouldn't mind it now."

"Well, they'd better not. They can call me Pinkey as much as they like, but they'd better let you alone, and a double fist beat into the air."

Richard laid a gentle hand on the clenched fist and stayed it in its course.

"Philip, you mustn't be like Simon Peter, he was always ready to fight for his Lord, but he couldn't stand the test of being still for him."

"What do you mean?"

"I mean, there is more strength needed to bear than to fight. The double fisted can't serve; it is the open hand that can really help. I've had lots of thoughts about these things, when I've been alone and could do nothing but think. Oh, Philip, I am sure the dear Lord has been trying all the time to make me understand."

Not altogether able to comprehend his companion's speech, Philip eased his mind by saying, "I'm glad folks don't die of good." Then Richard laughed and Philip laughed and the distance between was lessened by mental fellowship.

In these boy-calendars we find the record of the three years that have slipped by since our last visit to "Wiseman's Wildwood," and it is plainly evident that Trixey's school has been a success.

But where is Trixey, and what have the years measured out to her and Jack? It would take a book to tell it all and then you would have to get close to the Great Heart to appreciate the efforts of these young souls to liberate and lift; to bless and enlighten all their lives have touched. The proud and the rich, as well as the lowly, have visited them, and have been blessed, for "Wiseman's Wildwood" has become a synonym for heaven to the city outside. And Trixey? You will find her in her "throne room," sitting at the feet of Aunt Joy rehearsing the wonderful events that have taken place in her new home and Jack's. And such a fellow as Jack is! Why, you could fill a book with the wonderful things that Jack has done in his profession, and Trixey glows with pride and pleasure as she relates how Jack refused a case that promised him, Oh, ever so much! just because he was offered the wrong side of it, and how Jack persuaded another client not to take his case into court, but to put it into the hands of the Eternal Justice, and after it had worked out, Oh so wonderfully! he came around and give Jack a great big check, double what his fees would have been, and told him his advice had been worth a great deal more than that to him, for it had saved him his friends, his peace of mind and his faith in divine Justice. And so Trixey went on enumerating the virtues of her wonderful husband while Aunt Joy's heart drank in her sweet confidence and rejoiced in the harvest that had come from the sowing of these happy truths in the Day home when Trixey was a little girl.

Then followed more sacred passages from her life and Jack's. Aunt Joy softly stroked the shining hair of her niece and whispered ~ **"Blessed art thou among women"**. Trixey's head bowed for a moment on Aunt Joy's lap and then rising to her feet she stood before Aunt Joy, her soft clinging garments half revealing, half concealing the nature of her joy. Never has artist or poet expressed by brush or pen the divine Annunciation as did Trixey standing there with the tremulous light of a dawning realization radiating from her face and form, her eyes uplifted and her hands crossed upon her breast. Aunt Joy gazed upon her in silent adoration. Surely the "handmaid of the Lord" was never more divinely overshadowed.

A moment more the spell was broken, and Trixey flung herself into Aunt Joy's arms weeping out the emotions her soul could no longer control. A long silence followed and then Trixey's heart relieved itself in speech:

"It was a year ago when the dream first came to me. I thought I was sitting down by the little brook, when there arose from the water something that looked like a lily bud, and it floated toward me, the nearer it came the larger it grew and a strange joy filled me as I reached out my hand to take it, but before I

touched it the green calyx unfolded and a tiny child lay nestled within them. It was so beautiful my heart went out to it longing. I begged the lily to give it to me, but a voice like the rippling of the waters answered, 'Some day;' then I awoke, but life seemed so incomplete after that, and my former ideals imperfect, and go where I would the image of that beautiful child haunted me. Jack wondered at my abstraction and everybody noticed I was changed, but I could not seem to help it, nor for a time could I tell Jack what it was. At last one day we were alone down by the little stream, and then I told him of my dream and how I was haunted by the beauty of that child. Dear Jack, he is so wise and loving! He put his arm about me and said, 'Why, Trixey, that was only another ideal for us to realize. We may call that beautiful child to us from its home in the Infinite Love, God has bestowed upon us the power to do so, and if our hearts are one in their agreement to such consummation, our sacrament of love will be the vital magnet that shall draw to us the soul of that beautiful child.' Oh, it was all so wonderful the way Jack explained it, and then I understood the meaning of my dream and why it haunted me."

"Oh! Aunt Joy, such wonderful things have come to me since I have realized that it was given me to prepare a living garment for this beautiful expression of divine Love."

"I seem to know what Mary knew that kept her singing songs of ecstasy, and Jack and I have kept our bodies holy and our minds free from selfish thoughts, that we may become more worthy of our angel guest."

"And Oh, Aunt Joy, my dream is coming true, for nearer and nearer floating toward me on the stream of days, this beautiful child approaches, and 'some day' as the voice announced, the lily-bud will unfold for me."

CHAPTER VIII

THE COMING HOME OF LOVIE

*I*T IS JUNE. A FULL MOON HANGS OVER WISEMAN'S Wildwood; half in light half in shade, this spot of Nature holds its place like a redeeming thought in the heart of the great city.

There is an unwonted charm about the night that consecrates its beauty ~ a holy hush that holds you listening with the inner ear.

Oh, glorious night! Oh, wondrous night! Thy way from heaven to earth is filled with shining.

And angels of the Highest sing again that soundless Christmas song of glory and good will.

A star of promise shines above the woodland bungalow. The lights flash in and out of its windows. There is joy within its walls, for the Angle of Life waits to perform again the miracle of birth, and from its sanctuary of hiding comes forth a soul clad anew in the garments of pink and white infancy. Pain and fear have no part in its transit, for the glory of understood motherhood bars them out.

The shepherds and wise men have seen the star and heard the song, "Unto us a child is born."

Whosoever will may know that with every child born into the world heaven sings its song of glory and prepares for a Messiah.

Happy the father and mother who have learned the Divine Law through which they can co-operate with the Angel of Immortality and prepare for the coming soul such mental and physical garment as shall reveal and not conceal the God-likeness that is given them to clothe.

The curse is lifted from mankind when parentage is understood, when every father chooses his fatherhood and every mother her motherhood, and love and consideration are the ruling motives of each home.

Her dream is realized, the lily bud has unfolded for Trixey. The pink and white mystery that fed at the fountain of her happy life and shared her joyous heart-beats now nestles on her breast, a new-born babe. The exquisite joy of motherhood is hers. And only she who has shared it, knows what it means to clasp for the first time this bundle of divine humanity that fashioned 'neath her heart, and feel the miracle of Life manifest.

Lovie has Come

Hers is a triumphant entrance into existence, for her the laws of nature and of God have been sacredly obeyed. The tradition of Eve and the wisdom of men are brought to naught in her birth-chamber, for the harmonious ways of life have been trusted and pain and sorrow have no part in the coming of Lovie.

The light of Paradise glows throughout the pretty bungalow, for the door that swung wide at the entrance of Lovie remains ajar, and can never be closed to this household again.

Before she had been an hour on the planet Lovie opened a pair of wondering blue eyes upon the adoring group bending above her, and Jack declares she smiled. No one disputes him. If he had said she walked or talked, methinks the loving credulity of that little band of worshippers would have credited it nothing too wonderful for this heavenly marvel.

It was a new experience for the white-capped nurse in attendance. Never had she seen the conservative rules and regulations of a birth-chamber so utterly disregarded, and she afterward freed her mind on the matter to a fellow nurse after this manner:

"It was a queer proposition. I've no fault to find with them, they're lovely people all right, but all our training counts for nothing with such as they. Why, they don't even believe in sickness, and 'twas all that I could do to keep Mrs. Wiseman from getting up and dressing before her babe was an hour old. What do you think of that for a rational person? And then everybody about the house, grandfather and all, came trapesing in before I had the babe fairly dressed. I don't approve of such irregularities; they distract one.

"Dr. Maurice was there, but my! he stayed only a few minutes. He wasn't needed, and he said to me in the hall, 'They don't seem to have much use for our services!'"

"I could see by his looks he was very much disconcerted, and no wonder. I don't like to see people suffer, but I think it's right to follow out prescribed and orderly ways of life, though Mrs. Wiseman says, 'Every natural process ought to be as painless and easy as breathing, and would be if we were in perfect harmony with life."

Jack's father had come early in the evening, and catching the note of expectancy that thrilled the home-nest, he had sent his machine back to the stables and taken up his self-imposed watch beside **the picture** that almost meant a living presence to him now.

Jack came in and sat beside him for a little time, and they gazed together on that beloved face, and then the father spoke of the memories that were thronging his soul this night.

"It was just such a night as this, Jack," he said, "when you were born. Your mother came near giving her life for you, and a great fear possessed me lest I should lose her, for a few days I forgot all else in my solicitude for her. I stayed by her bedside day and night. How well I remember, it made her so happy to have me near her, for we loved each other dearly, Jack. But when the danger was past, in my blindness and selfishness I went back to my money-getting, and applied myself to it closer than ever **for my boy's sake**. In my short-sightedness I deceived myself into believing the accumulation of wealth was the greatest thing I could do for you and her, and so missed my chances for making you happy with my presence and sympathy. You know the rest of the story, but I did not realize till too late what I had done. Oh, my son, I would give all I ever possessed to be able to restore to that face (pointing to the picture) the look of joy and happiness my thoughtless selfishness has denied it."

A great sob burst from his tortured soul. Jack's arms were about his father, and a mighty love poured itself out upon them, while he reviewed to his remorseful parent the many beautiful things he had done since they had taken up their abode in the little bungalow, and how Trixey could never find praises enough for his sweet attention to all that concerned the new home and its inmates. And further, that he knew **she** (the invisible mother) felt and understood, too, the change that had come, and their joys were hers. The father's soul was comforted, and when an hour later he looked down upon the little pink vision of Lovie, a peace came over him, and he felt as if **she** might be standing beside him knowing the fullness of his heart, and a fervent "Thank God!" went forth unconsciously from his lips, which led Trixey to reach up and kiss him. Those looking saw a face transfigured, for the glory from the "door ajar" shone about him and the walls of separation were dissolved.

To Aunt Joy waiting in the white silence of Trixey's "throne room" returned like a dream, the remembrance of a night like this when the Angel of Life knocked at her door and the sweet joys of motherhood were bestowed upon her.

Oh, if she had only **known** then what she knows now, the gladness of her sacred trust would not have been blighted by fear and solicitude over the health of her delicate boy. How that little body-temple might have glowed with the fullness of Life! Oh, if she had only **known** how her own fear and anxiety barred it out, where her faith and trust could have kept the doors wide swung to life. But Aunt Joy is not the one to let useless regret weaken the power of her present activity for good, and her soul rejoiced and gave thanks for the knowledge that made her free. And later on as she bent above the young Madonna and child, she felt that heaven and earth had conspired to do their harmonious best for the coming of Lovie.

CHAPTER IX

BABYHOOD

*T*O THE BABE SLUMBERING UNDER THE CREAMY COVER OF her down crib it seemed of little moment that the sun was rising on her first earth-day. And to that great luminary spreading the east with morning splendor, what could it possibly matter that the night-angel had unfolded this dainty bit of humanity, slumbering under the creamy cover of her downy crib? But we are calculating outside the charmed circle of the pretty bungalow to assume indifference of this kind, for to the quickening sense of the new joy felt there, the whole universe seemed in sympathy.

It was with certainty these happy souls looked out upon the glowing east as a demonstration of the joy that thrilled the golden heart of day because of this babe slumbering under the creamy cover of the downy crib. Was it not a contribution to the **Great-All** ~ this slumbering babe that had come in the night, clothed in the vestments of humanity?

Why should not the great sun give heed and rejoice that a pair of blue eyes had unfolded and a new life had come to share in his warmth and glory?

Why should not the skies bend lower and the air grow softer because of this nestling, trusting little life that asks of them the alms of breath?

Why should not the little wood take on brighter color and the wood-folk greater joy, because of this little life that is to bring them such companionship as was never theirs before? And so the birds sang and the creatures frisked as never before, while the bees and butterflies winging about, told to the listening flowers the tale of the babe they saw nestled under the creamy covers of her downy crib in the pretty bungalow.

Heaven and earth were so blended in the happy consciousness of the young father and mother whose sweet, new treasure slumbered in the downy crib that Trixey said, "Dear Jack, how are we ever to tell where heaven leaves off and earth begins in our new blessedness?"

It was a strong, assuring voice that answered as Jack's lips touched those of the ecstatic young mother:

"Why, Trixey, sweetheart, God never intended us to divide ourselves between two worlds. Heaven and earth are only divorced from each other because of mankind's failure to perceive God's great unity. Heaven and earth were as husband and wife till ignorance and superstition separated them. They were joined together in the beginning, and it was written as in the marriage vow: **'What God hath joined together, let no man put asunder.'**"

"Oh, Jack," said Trixey putting her arms about his neck, "I see as never before, what the first great mistake was that turned Adam and Eve out of their Eden and gave to their children such unhappy portion, but we, dear Jack will always remember in ours to listen to 'the voice walking in the garden' and to obey it and never eat of the fruit of the dual tree."

"A noble resolve, my blessed girl, and that those of our household may practice it with us, I will have painted upon the wall of every room, this reminder:

> ### 𝕲-o-d
> ### In all and through all and above all.
> ### The one Power and one Presence

For a while there was silence in the pretty chamber, for these two souls were absorbed in the contemplation of that Presence that walked unhindered in their midst and whose silent voice was more sweet to them than any sound ear ever heard, and they were realizing as never before that all the joy and beauty that had come to them was but God expressing himself more visibly to their consciousness.

Jack's voice broke the silence and his eyes were upon the slumbering babe as he spoke, "Trixey, sweetheart, how wonderfully we have been led up to this great climax. I am remembering with blessings every little help on the way. I can see now where I was blind before, that in those experiences which I pronounced **evil,** Adam-like, I separated myself from companionship with the All-Good. Now I am redeeming my word by blessing even those darkest hours of my boy-life, and it has cleared my spiritual sight so I can see the strength and knowledge that were born of that solitude. But for that experience this blessed wildwood might not have been ours now—for it was my loneliness that drove me here, and then it grew so sacred I could not part with it, because of the invisible companionship I felt when I came here. I thought it was my mother's presence then, but now I know 'tis God's; and, too, I know 'twas leading me to find what I have found in you and this sweet home—and now our darling child. If you and I have realized so much, what may not this little one realize, who from her first inception has been fed on thoughts of God?" Trixey's hand stole into her husband's and together they talked of the wonderful possibilities of the slumbering babe.

it was then that Trixey told of her beautiful experience with this child that was to come from out of the glad days to them. Whenever she had been out in the wildwood alone, Trixey said, like a presence walking hand-in-hand with her, was this beautiful child ~ she could not see it with her outer eyes, but she **felt** its gladness and beauty; felt its childish voice as it prattled with the little stream and sang with the birds. But most she felt its glad delight when under the big oak, or drinking in the woodsey fragrance of the early morning, or watching the nesting birds. She was quite sure the little presence was visible to all the woods folk, for they came so close and looked so intently; and one day a white pigeon hovered above her and settled for a moment, as if on the head of the invisible child, and she felt it was a benediction of peace upon them both. Jack did not smile at these queer fancies; he only said, "Dear little girl, how lovely!" for he had a theory that the soul of the unborn child sought companionship, and in the quiet of the little wood, she had become receptive to it.

But Lovie was a visible presence now, slumbering beside them in her downy crib, and the happy mother knew that some day they would roam together the little forest hand-in-hand, as the dream-child had done.

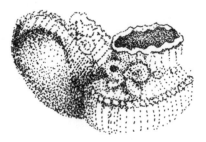

Lovie's blue eyes opened upon her seventh earth-day and a surprise party at the same time, but not being versed in the customs of this planet, she only blinked at the three boys hanging over her crib trying to attract her attention to the gifts that had cost them one whole week's careful saving, for Lovie had not yet come to a sense of appreciation for the gay jumping jack that Pinkey, **alias** Philip, swung temptingly before her, neither had she felt the necessity that should make practical the smooth white teething ring that Crutches, **alias** Richard, tried to put into her little fist. Nor had the pink rubber ball, which Pigeontoe, **alias** Henry, bounced up and down, any merit for her. No, Lovie was just a week-old baby, and it mattered not to her that these boys were disappointed in her, nor that Pinkey said, "I never thought **she'd be like that**. I went to see Miss Hunt's baby a-purpose to find out what babie's like. But, my! Miss Hunt's baby wasn't that way; it was crawlin' all over the floor, and just crazy for jumpin' jacks and things."

Lovie's babyhood was sweet and free and natural as a bird's. Her little body was never pinched and tortured by the abominations custom has imposed upon the innocent babe in the way of wardrobe. Her wise friends assumed that her perfect little form could retain its beauty, its symmetry, its freedom of growth, by being clad in loose, light garments, and so Lovie was dressed for comfort and not for display, though her dainty gowns would have satisfied the most artistic eye.

Sunshine and air and water she had a-plenty and reasonable service from her loving friends, but never into Lovie's baby-life was dropped a suggestion of fear or evil. She never knew there was anything to hurt or be afraid of and so her sweet babyhood unfolded like a lovely blossom, and her young life rippled on in perpetual joy.

CHAPTER X.
HER FIRST BIRTHDAY

*L*OVIE HAD SUCCESSFULLY CARRIED OUT THE CHARMING programme of sweet baby-hood for a whole year without encountering one of the nursery phantoms that beset the fear-ridden home. Her cooings had never been interrupted by physical inharmony, nor her slumbers disturbed because of the little pearls so lovingly slipped into the pink casket of her mouth by the Bountiful Giver.

Baby Lovie had never been deprived of her natural birthright of health and harmony, for no one ever talked error in her sweet world, and no one trusted other than the presence of Love and Wisdom in that peaceful home, and so God walked unhindered in her budding life, and like the Child of long ago, she "grew and waxed strong in spirit, filled with wisdom and the grace of God."

It was a rare pleasure to witness the unfolding of this uninterrupted soul, for with Lovie the sweet naturalness of the child was blended with that ineffable **something** before which humanity bows and to which art lends a halo.

When, in celebration of Lovie's first birthday, Trixey took her by the hand and led her toddling steps through the little forest, she was wild in her delight. She buried her baby face in the fragrant grasses; she kissed and patted the brown tree trunks; she fluttered her little arms after the flying birds; she prattled to the frisking squirrels, and when they stopped beside the running stream she clapped her tiny hands and dipped them into the water, while her silvery laugh rang out, a new and wholesome chord in the sweet noises of the wood.

It was a wonderful day. Out under the big oak a banquet was served in honor of it, and the three boys were bidden guests. You should have seen Lovie. She showed herself a royal hostess, patting the three urchins with her baby hands and assuring them in sweet and tender ways of a cordial welcome.

We will not attempt a menu of this feast. Janie had spared no pains in the decoration of the birthday cake, and had filled it with surprises, known only to herself and Lovie's stately grandfather. So that when Philip and Richard and Henry were given their pieces, they found a golden coin in each. Janie beamed all over at this disclosure. Jack and Trixey looked their surprise. A good, glad laugh followed the explanation, and the three boys could hardly believe their eyes as they saw the golden eagles shining in their brown hands. Janie gave them each a purse to hold their treasure, and no millionaire ever felt richer than they.

When they had recovered from their surprise, Trixey returned to them the gifts they had tried to bestow upon the irresponsive babe of a week, with the instruction that they were to present them again at this ~ Lovie's first birthday.

A rustic throne had been constructed for the little queen under the big oak, and here she sat in state when Philip approached with his gift. He hesitated, his face changed color under the stress of conflicting thoughts, for Philip was not quite sure it was "honor bright to fool 'er that way," as he afterward said. So he cleared his conscience by this explanation:

"I know, Miss Lovie, you'se only a little bit of girl, but I'll be fair and square with you just the same, and won't give this thing o'er again without tellin' you I brung it for you a year ago. You's awful little then and didn't know much, so you ma kept 'em and let us do it over again. Its name is jack-in-a-box, and when you push this way, he jumps out," and suiting the action to the word, out jumps jack to the great delight of Lovie, who clapped her hands and cried, "**M-o-e, m-o-e,**" every time jack went back into the box. Then Philip showed her little hands how to press the spring, and poor jack-in-the-box got no rest for the next ten minutes. The enthusiasm of the one-year-old Lovie was surely sufficient to make amends for the indifference shown by the week-old baby, and the boys were satisfied.

The white teething ring presented by Richard afforded her entertainment for a season, and then Henry's pink ball was given a trial. When Lovie discovered she could toss it on the grass, and keep the three boys rolling over each other in their efforts to return it to her, she kept them busy till her attention was diverted by the chirping and chattering going on under the hickory, where a banquet had been spread for the wood-fold from the fragments of her birthday feast. The birds and squirrels were having a merry time over it, for there were plenty of nuts as well as crumbs on the white cloth spread under the

 tree. Lovie's little heart felt the importance of making those other guests welcome, and so she clambered down from her rustic throne and toddled over to them. She sat down among the feasters with the greatest composure. Her presence created a little flurry at first, but the creature-folk were soon satisfied of her good intentions, and were not long in accepting the dainty morsels her dimpled hand held out to them.

The party under the big oak were watching with loving interest the proceeding under the hickory, when Jack discovered his father had slipped in among them unnoticed, and was as much absorbed in the little drama as the rest of them.

Lovie and feathered friends were getting very intimate. One little sparrow was tugging at the blue ribbon in her hair, which he evidently fancied. Two others were nestling on her shoulder, while the food scattered over the cloth had been discarded for the tempting bits dealt out by her little hands. It was a pretty sight, and Lovie worked hard to keep up with the demand.

Suddenly there was a shrill chirp, a whir of wings, and Lovie's feathered friends were in the air, while across the white cloth glided a dark, sinuous form that made the boys spring to their feet and the stately grandfather turn livid.

Instantly Jack stayed them with his hand, and quietly commanded everyone to sit down and keep still. "It is only another of our wood friends come to the birthday party; there is no danger whatever. The child is perfectly safe," he calmly said.

Then laying his hand on Trixey's, which was trembling slightly, he continued softly, "There is nothing to fear, sweetheart, for we know there is but One Life pulsating these little woods and that belongs alike to every living creature, which makes it sacred as well as common to us all, and we love and bless it in all its forms, even in yonder reptile."

All had resumed their sitting posture at Jack's command, though with great effort as they beheld that subtle thing glide near the precious hand that reached out to it a bit of the birthday cake.

Would this awful moment ever be done with? Lovie's proffered hospitality passed unaccepted by her strange guest, but as if to show comradeship, the snake coiled itself in the grass beside her, greatly to the delight of Lovie, who put out her little hand and softly patted its shining coils.

"My God!" groaned the frantic grandfather. "I can stand this no longer; get a gun, Jack, and end this reptile before he fastens his fangs into our baby."

Jack's face was calm and fearless as he made answer, "Father, there never has been a gun in these woods since my time; every creature here has my protection. The child is perfectly safe ~ see! they are friends, even a snake appreciates confidence and love, and that serpent coiled up yonder beside our babe is as innocent of doing her an injury as she is of harming him.

"We have put enmity between ourselves and certain creatures and hunted them down, and made ourselves believe we were doing it for self-protection, when in reality we were only sacrificing them to our ignorance and fear. It is we, and not the creature-world, that are responsible for the feud set up between us. If we would exercise the love and trust of that child, there is not a living creature in all this world would do us harm.

"Have you not read of how the mothers of India leave their babes under the trees while at their labor, and though poisonous serpents crawl all around them it is said there has never been one bitten? It is not until a child arrives at the age or state of mind that seeks self-defense that he is ever molested by them. 'Love never faileth.' God's creatures always respond to the God-quality in man."

As Jack finished he gave a soft, warbling whistle, which was known to Lovie as "papa's play call." She looked up and answered the signal with a little wave of her hand, then she clambered to her feet, while her strange companion uncoiled and glided swiftly into the grass.

The strain was over. Tears followed the stately grandfather's pallor. Trixey breathed a fervent "Thank God!" The three boys looked at each other in speechless astonishment for a moment, and then, unable to control the reaction of their feelings, threw up their hats with a whoop and hurrah!

Then with one accord they all rushed to meet the little heroine. The mother caught her to her heart; the father tossed her high in the air; the grateful grandfather kissed her with shining eyes, and put in her hand a precious birthday packet; while the boys declared **she was a peach.**

CHAPTER XI.
A LEAF FROM
MAMA TRIXEY'S DIARY

Lovie was a regular wood nymph. The little steam told her wonderful stories. The grass and trees, the birds and skies, all had a language for her, and so when the rainy days came and shut her in the pretty bungalow, Mama Trixey taxed her ingenuity to take the place of the outdoor companionship. And so it came about that when the rain made a whole week's visit to the little forest, and Lovie wanted to know about "when you'se a little girl, mama," that Trixey brought out a queer old bundle of soiled and yellow papers and to Lovie's delight, told her that these were some of mama's stories when she was a little girl, which she had told to the paper instead of the birds and trees. And so Lovie never tired of listening about what mama and Grace and Aunt Joy and all of 'em did, when mama was a little girl. It was the story of Tom Sams and Janie Smith that interested her most, because Tom and Janie were members of their household, and this is what the story said, and just like her mama was a little girl and telling it:

We'ver had some funny things happen to us, Ned and I, 'cause some way, after saying the **words** Aunt Joy gave us last week, we don't seem to think like we used to.

Papa got after Ned for being seen on the street with Tom Sams, 'cause he's called the baddest boy in town. And papa seemed cross to me, too. 'cause he saw Janie Smith here the other day, and he told me if I couldn't find a more 'spectable girl to entertain than her, I couldn't have company.

Aunt Joy asked papa to read Luke vi chapter for the morning lesson, and told us to be sure and listen very carefully.

So papa read it. I remember most it said, you must love folks that didn't love you, and be good to 'em and give 'em everything they asked for, and then you'd be called the children of the Highest, 'cause He's kind to the unthankful and evil, and we must be that way, just like our Father is.

Then papa prayed that we might heed and practice this lesson.

When he was through, Ned went up and put his arms 'round papa's neck and asked him if he didn't want us to be children of the Highest.

Papa said: "Certainly, I do."

"Then," Ned said, "didn't you read, 'He is kind to the evil?' Now papa, that's just what I was trying to be to Tom Sams. I was going along the street when he yelled out, as he always does, 'Hello, three legs, where's your third foot?' But I've been saying for a week, 'I can have no unkind thought, for my Father is Love;' so I didn't feel a bit cross at him, but just turned and said: 'Now you've taken the trouble to ask, I'll tell you. My **third** leg grew on a tree and I didn't get the **foot**.' Then he laughed and called me 'jolly,' and said it was too bad I had to wear a crutch."

"He kept walking along with me and told me he hoped I wouldn't mind the way he'd talked to me, for he'd got to doin' them things 'cause folks was down on him so, and called him mean, even when he tried to be good."

"He told me lots of things he'd done, real brave things, but 'cause 'twas him, they said he meant mischief."

"Then I just told him I didn't mind anything he'd ever said to me, 'cause now I knew him I knew he was good, and I loved him. He asked what kind of taffy I was feedin' him. I told him 'twas the kind our Father feeds us all on ~ **love**. Then I told him how happy I was now, that I loved everybody."

"He said, 'I believe you; but say, ain't you afraid you're gettin' so good you'll die?'"

"Then I laughed, it was so funny, the way he said it, and looked. That was just as you passed papa, in the carriage with Deacon Jones. I told him folks didn't die of good. And then I couldn't help but tell him all about our lesson of the seed and flower Aunt Joy gave us."

"He seemed to understand it, too, for he said if folks 'ud just quit tramping on 'im, he believed the good would sprout in him, too."

Papa kissed Ned.

Then I told papa why Janie Smith had been here, and how I'd always disliked her in school, 'cause she looked dirty, and how she'd always make faces at me and called me "stuck up," and I'd thought her real mean and told teacher on her. But after I'd said, "God my Father is good, and I am good," some way, I couldn't feel ugly to her any more, but just put out my hand and said, "Janie, let's be friends." She stood and looked at me till I said, "Janie, can't you **like** me?" and then she just cried and said she always wanted to like me, but I wouldn't let her 'cause she's poor and dirty. Then she told me her mother was always sick, and she did ever'thing hers'f, and couldn't fix up nice and clean, but she'd like to. So I had her come home with me, and Aunt Joy fixed her up in some of my clothes and she looked so nice and happy and good, I wondered how I could ever think she was mean.

Papa looked like tears; he put his face in his hands and sat awhile, then he said: "I have just read, 'Why call ye me Lord,

Lord, and do not the things that I say?' Joy, I stand rebuked by these children. How have you gotten this gospel into such perfect action with them?"

Aunt Joy said, "Except ye become as one of them, ye cannot know. now, children, give your papa the lesson that has taught you these truths."

So we told papa all about the seed and flower, and the words we have said this week. But papa couldn't understand how saying these words could make us do them.

Aunt Joy said, "I told you, brother, 'except ye become as a little child, ye cannot understand these mysteries.'"

Then papa said, "Grace, how can I get little?"

Grace laughed and said: "Oh, papa, you can't make your legs little, or your head little; you des make your finks little."

"But you don't help me one bit, baby, for how am I to make my 'thinks' little?"

"Let go all the big finks, and keep **one** little fink, like the little f'owers do."

"Well, what **think** is that?"

"Little seed always 'members about the f'ower."

"Well, baby, what is my flower, and how can I remember, too?"

"Oh, God's your f'ower, His little **know** is in you."

"Joy, what **is** this child trying to get at?" asked papa.

"That everything bringeth forth seed of its kind," said Aunt Joy. " 'One is **your** father, even God. Whosoever is born of

God, doth not commit sin; for **His** seed remaineth in him; and he cannot sin, because he **is** born of God.' 'Be ye therefore perfect, even as your Father in heaven is perfect.' "

"But, Joy, do you mean to teach these children that **they** can become **like** God?"

"If we accept Jesus Christ's doctrine, what else can we teach? Spirit is ever the Father of Spirit; Spirit is ever the Son of Spirit. God is Spirit. 'He that honoreth not the Son, honoreth not the Father which sent him; for the Father loveth the Son, and showeth him all things that Himself doeth.' 'I and the Father are one,' said Christ. And we are told, 'Let this mind be in you, which was in Christ Jesus, who, being in the form of God, thought it not robbery to be equal with God.'"

"But you must remember the same authority says, 'He took upon himself the form of a servant, and was made in the likeness of men, and became obedient unto death.'"

"Yes, God created man in His **own** image, and pronounced him **good**. 'The Word was made flesh,' and the Father said, 'This is my beloved Son, in whom I am well pleased,' ~ **manifest man**, working as the Father worketh. 'As the Father hath life in Himself, so hath He given the Son life in Himself.' To prove the truth of this, Jesus Christ laid down His **manifest** life, and took it up again, and declared to all, 'He that hath the Son hath life.'"

"What do you understand that to mean?"

"The same as 'the light that lighteth' ~ **Being** ~ what Grace calls the '**know**.' 'No man cometh unto the Father but by me (the Son).' 'Because I live, ye shall live also; at that day ye shall know that I am in my Father and ye in me and I in you.' '**That**

day' always means the time of realization."

"Trixey," said papa, "do you understand what Aunt Joy means by 'having the mind that was in Christ Jesus'?"

"Yes," I said, "I have the mind that was in Christ Jesus; because Christ Jesus was my Father's obedient child, and I am His obedient child."

"How do you know?"

"Cause He's good and I'm good; He loves, and I love."

"What makes you think you're good?"

" 'Cause I think everybody's good, and I'm one of 'em."

"What! when they do bad things?"

"Well, we thought Tom and Janie were mean and bad till we knew 'em, and I guess it would be just the same with everybody, when we come to know 'em."

Aunt Joy said, "He that walketh righteously and speaketh uprightly, and shutteth his eyes from seeing evil, shall dwell on high."

Papa said, "Joy, the results of your teaching are beautiful. Still, I can't help fearing these children are getting loose ideas of Christ and God."

"Christ told you judge of a tree by its fruits," said Aunt Joy. "Here you say the fruits are figs, but you fear the tree is a thistle. 'Do men gather figs of thistles?' Come, what is the fruit of your thinking? Suspicious of your own children, even when they are fulfilling the only law Christ recognized ~ **Love.** Fearing to claim kinship with the beloved Son, when it is declared 'He that abideth in the doctrine of Christ, he hath both the Father and the Son.' Also, 'We are in him that is true, even in His Son, Jesus Christ.' This is the true God, and eternal life."

"Grace," said papa, "who is the true God and Jesus Christ?"

"Oh," said Grace, pointing, "He's here and ever'where, and He lives in the happy little spot right in here, and nuffin', nuffin' can get the happy out or hurt Grace, 'cause the little **know** sees Him all the time. The little **know** is Jesus the Son ~ des like the seed's **know**."

> No sooner did the sunshiny weather crown the little wood again than Lovie was out telling to all the creature-folk the wonderful stories her "little-girl-mother telled on paper."
>
> The old oak and the listening birds heard it over and over, and could have told you all about Grace and Ned, Tom and Janie, Aunt Joy and the Day family.
>
> The little brook laughed and gurgled, and, Lovie said, "Clapped its hands, because it was so glad about the lovely stories little mama telled, and because the Great Love put it into the heart of Tom Sams to make a place for it here where Mama Trixey and God lives."

CHAPTER XII

SEVEN TIMES ONE

*S*EVEN SUMMERS HAVE GARNERED THEIR GOLDEN sunlight; seven autumns lighted their torches of flame; seven winters hung with pearl and ermine the little forest, and seven springtimes pitched green tents there, since the coming of Lovie.

It is the first of June, and Lovie is seven times one today. The soul of the little wood is all aglow with expectancy, for there are to be a hundred little guests at Lovie's birthday party.

The big oak and the creature-folk have talked it all over with Lovie, for she has told them again and again the story of these "sunless children," that the little girl in the park related to her, and she feels the great loving sympathy of all the wood respond to her deep compassion for these little ones who have never had trees, nor flowers, nor birds, nor grass in all their lives, nor sunshine in their dark homes way, way down in the big, big city. The little girl said so, and the little girl knew, because she lived down there herself.

Of course, everything will help make this the very happiest day that ever dawned. Lovie is sure of that, for her own little heart is so full of it. In the whispering of the big oak she hears the promise: "I will make of my branches loving

arms of protection for these dear children," And in the chirp of the red-bibbed robin, the assurance ~"I will sing, cheer, cheer to them all the day long." And the chatter of the cunning squirrel to her is the merry declaration: "I will whisk and frisk and wave my bushy tail to make them happy."

And even the fragrant grass seemed promising: "I will make it cool and soft for their tiny feet."

And so all things are Lovie's happy confederates.

The contagion of her supreme desire to make happiness for these little guests has spread over the city, so that there is no end to offers of automobiles and other conveyances for the transportation of these tenement children to Wiseman's Wildwood. But Lovie is not aware of all this, nor the transformation that has taken place in her little guests since the boys found them in the dirty street.

Never was more thorough scrubbing, combing and clipping done to any youngsters, than these received at kindly hands of motherly women, who offered their services to help along. And, Oh! the delight of these children when put into new and pretty garments provided through the loving thought of Lovie's grandfather. You never would have guessed from this how displeased he was when Jack and Trixey first told him of Lovie's desire to have these children come to her birthday party. Why! the old proud spirit fairly blazed in him at the thought of his darling entertaining the slums; but we'll omit the record of those things, for **only the good is true**, and we want the true only. Jack and Trixey were silent, for they knew he would see it altogether different when Lovie presented the subject to him, and it was so. A little later Lovie, with one hand on her grandfather's shoulder, and with face pressed close to his, was telling him about these little sunless children, 'way, ever-so-far down in the big city, and how more than anything else in all the world she wanted them to come to her pretty wood, where the sun could shine upon them through the cool green leaves and the trees could whisper to them and the grass and flowers kiss their dear feet and make their hearts so happy they'd never, never forget it in all their lives.

There was something irresistible in Lovie's manner of putting the case. The child's soul had conceived a truth that had something more in it than a day of pleasure for these sunless, loveless children ~ there was a demand in it that plowed deep into the heart of her proud grandfather, and turned up fertile soil there. The seeds of a new consciousness sprang up within him. It was as if he were given to see what this child had conceived, **the kinship of all humanity**; as if his great love for her must include love for all children. The accident of birth seemed a vain trifle to him now. Children were children, whatever their environment, and demanded love and care to bring out the divine in them. But we are not going to spy into the new intentions that have set his soul afire in the last thirty minutes; we will be content with watching the outcome. Of course Lovie was promised all she had asked, and more too. And as she put her little arms about her grandfather's willing neck and kissed him over and over, she assured him he was the very dearest fadder-grand that any little girl could have. It was Lovie's own sweet way of always addressing him as fadder-grand, with accent on the **grand,** and a very appropriate title it seemed for that stately gentleman.

When Lovie led her transformed grandfather into Trixey's pretty boudoir, and joyously announced to her father and mother what she and "fadder-grand" were going to do, there was a merry twinkle in Jack's eyes, but he only said, "A little child shall lead them."

"Yes," answered his sire with face aglow, "A little child has more power than a king on his throne, for within the last half hour this one has wrought a miracle in me, I know not how, but I am as one delivered from a great darkness. I think I must be ready for your new humanity. Jack and Trixey expressed their delight, but Lovie apparently oblivious of all else, stood surveying her grandfather with that look that takes no account of flesh and blood. Then a radiance came into her face, and she exclaimed, "Oh, fadder-grand, it's gone, it's gone, it's light, it's light all over, there used to be a place that didn't shine, but now, fadder-grand, it shines," and the child rushed into his arms and buried her face in his bosom. It was the habit of Lovie to describe people as light and dark. There was no good and bad to her; it was all light and darkness, according as the spirit shone out or was obscured.

After leaving Lovie, Mr. Wiseman, who was now thoroughly alive to the spirit of the occasion, summoned to his aid the three boys whom we first knew, as Pinkey, Pigeontoe and Crutches; but after as Philip, Henry and Richard, grown now into youths of industry and promise.

Small wonder these boys were only too familiar with the districts from which Lovie's birthday guests were to be gathered, and that they should enter heartily into the plan for securing for these desolate children a happy holiday.

It was with reluctance that they consented to let Mr. Wiseman accompany them on this expedition into the slums of the city; they wanted to spare him. But Lovie's grandfather was not to be spared anything. A desire had been born in him to know the bare facts concerning these uncanny districts, and for reasons of his own he was determined to do so.

Philip naturally took the lead and designated "Kid's Row," as a starter. "For," as he explained, "there used to be more kids to the square inch here than you could shake a stick at. Women who couldn't get about, used to keep 'em while their mothers worked or wandered. I was one of them myself once. Nights we's packed so thick on the floor you couldn't step." And then as these past recollections rushed over him, Philip's voice took on eloquent pathos as he continued, "And, Oh, Mr. Wiseman, none but those who have felt it can know what it means to be poor in a big city. If it hadn't been for that little woods and Mr. Jack and Mrs. Wiseman, I suppose we'd been slumming it yet, and Richard a cripple."

What volumes were contained in Philip's simple statement! There were thoughts set going in this multi-millionaire's mind that boded much, for surely if a little wholesome association and training could raise these three boys out of the slums into useful manhood, it were far better to provide for such, than to punish for crimes that need never be.

So while the boys were piloting Mr. Wiseman through scenes we have no desire to transcribe, he beheld in the dirty, ragged, haggard children that were to be Lovie's birthday guests, the innocent victims of such environment; and almost instantaneously, with the thought of helping them, came the tormenting remembrance that one of his agents had told him of a foreclosure "on some rotten property" somewhere in this locality. What if this should be it, and he should prove to be the legal landlord of these awful tenements? The thought was sickening, and he hid his face in his hands, unable to gaze upon what might be the product of his own avarice. The boys, taking note of this strange action, thought the unwholesome air had affected him, and urged him to return to his waiting machine. But no, Lovie's grandfather, more than ever, determined to face it out. Some day it will be different here. **Some day**; but we'll leave that for him to work out.

But 'tis Lovie's birthday, and loving, motherly hands have cleansed these little ones and gowned them in pretty new dresses, provided by "an unknown friend," and wonderful wagons without horses came and whirled them away into the sunshine and out into a world of beauty. They live in that short ride a life-time of enjoyment. Children of the sunlight can never know what this delicious whirl through sunshine and fresh air meant to those children of the tenements.

And then to be put down in such a wonder-world as Wiseman's Wildwood! Some of the children who had heard of heaven thought they were there, and others who had in some way learned of fairyland were sure this was it. And when they discovered Lovie in her bower of roses under the big oak waiting for them, some thought "angel" and some "fairy." But one little girl, unable to restrain her feelings, cried out, "Oh her's a fairy, her's a fairy, for I've seen 'em in pictures." When the boys brought them close to Lovie you could feel the children hold their breath in admiration and wonder, for Lovie put out her hands and welcomed them in a way they had never known before. And something grew light within them, and this radiant little girl made them feel that they were like her, and she told them of the trees and birds and flowers. And they sat down on the soft green grass and listened, and the trees whispered to them and the birds sang to them and the sun shone for them, and all the day long there was joy and gladness everywhere in that little wood for these happy visiting children.

And O, the feast and the flowers! It would take volumes to tell all that day had in it for Lovie and her little guests. And when the wonderful day came to a close and the children were whirled away home again, every one was laden with sweets and flowers, and better still, in each little heart shone a light Lovie had kindled there, that could never, never be extinguished.

CHAPTER XIII.

CHRISTMASTIDE

*W*INTER'S WHITE STILLNESS IS OVER THE LITTLE FOREST. The Wisemans have just returned from abroad, and Lovie is having her first taste of winter in the Wildwood. A shout of joy heralds her arrival, and a little later her snow boots are plowing through the unbroken white of the little wood. Merrily she pushes forward for a season, and then stops short and casts a look of uncertainty about, for a strange world confronts her. Where are her trees and shrubs and running stream?

Tall brown columns stretch up and spread sprangly fingers against the gray overhead. Queer shapes hooded in white cluster about, and thrust dark arms toward her. It is a sign of friendliness to Lovie, and she puts out her mittened hand and touches the one nearest ~ it feels very like her old friend, the bitter-sweet; one hearty shake and the hood falls off. A little "Oh!" escapes the astonished child, for there stands poor little bittersweet without even so much as a leaf to hide the nakedness of her brown quivering limbs from the freezing cold. Lovie

throws her warm arms as far around the naked bush as they will reach and whispers, "It won't be long to wait, Sweetie, spring is coming soon and you'll have lots of pretty clothes, and the birds will be back and your little empty nests will all be full again," Then something seemed to stir deep down in the being of the little bush, and whisper back to her:

"I'm not up there in the cold; I'm down here in the heart of the earth, where wood-life gathers 'round its winter's hearthstone."

"And what do you do?" whispered the child.

"Oh," answered the tiny voice, "we listen and tell each other."

"Tell what?" asked Lovie so loud that the tiny voice was lost. Letting go of the bush she turned to find her father looking down upon her.

"What new discovery is the little girl making now?" he asked as she turned her eager face to him.

"Oh," she said, "if only **it** would tell me the rest."

Her father smiled questioningly, while Lovie put her arms once more around the little bush, but no voice answered. Then she explained, "It talked once, Papa-Jack;" and then followed the question, "Where do trees keep their **alive** in the winter?"

In answer, Papa-Jack put his hands under the arms of the little maiden and lifted her to his broad shoulders, and then plowed his way over to the big oak. Lovie was expectant, for Papa-Jack always chose the big oak for his "story place" when they were in the little wood. So when he let her down gently and stood her on the white snow, and asked her that she look up and see how far the great brown branches reached, she knew something very interesting would follow, and it did. Papa-Jack told how the great root-branches of the big oak reached down into the brown earth as far beneath them as the leaf-branches did above, and how they drank in the sweet waters of hidden springs, and ate up the very rocks to make tall and strong the body of the great oak. It was all very wonderful, this tale of the "alive" of the big oak, and when it came to where the living sap went down into the big under chambers of the root-branches to get away from the freezing cold, and live through the winter, Lovie clapped her hands and cried out, "Just like the bittersweet bush said. They are all down there around their winter's fire telling wonderful, wonderful stories. Why can't we hear their stories, too, Papa-Jack?"

"We could, dear, if we were still enough, but people have believed so long that they hear with their ears, that the real hearer is forgotten, and so we hear but little of the great anthems of life."

"Let's listen, then," exclaimed the little child, putting her ear close to the rough bark of the oak. There was silence for the next five minutes, and then Lovie spun round with her hands over her ears, exclaiming, "It's awfully funny; it tickles my ears, and makes me feel just like doing this way," and round and round she spun again. "Now you try it, Papa-Jack."

So Papa-Jack gravely put his hear to the big tree, and heard with his mind something he had not remembered for a long time. Then he rapped with his knuckles on the rough bark and called out, "Central please give me 12000 Oak."

Lovie's laugh rang out merrily, but Papa-Jack continued gravely, "Is this 12000 Oak? Yes? Is little Miss Bittersweet there? If perfectly convenient I would like to speak with her." Without noticing Lovie's merriment, Papa-Jack went on with his 'phoning. "Hello, is this you, Miss Bittersweet? Would you mind telling us the story that is interesting the wood-folk down there at this season? Is that so? How wonderful! You too are telling the story of Christmas? What do you know of Christmas away down there? Only holly and evergreen have to do with Christmas up here. What's that? You have a Christmas story of your own? Won't you please tell it to us? Thank you. I will repeat it after you so that I may be sure of getting it correctly. There, I'm ready. Proceed."

Lovie was close by her father's side now listening attentively while Papa-Jack repeated Bittersweet's story.

"When the great sun goes to the Southland, and the winter king comes to his icy throne, we wood-folk leave our homes up in the light land and come down here. It is dark here, but we are warm and safe, and happy. We rest, and sleep and dream the time away until about the 25th of December. Then the sudden thrill of the great sun's coming north sets all our pulses going, and baby Spring is born to us here in the manger of earth. We are full of glad rejoicing because she is the child of light, and will bring us back to the world of sunshine and blossoms. Long, long ago people used to be glad with us, and make feasts and give presents because baby Spring was being born down here on the 25th of December. You have it different now up there; you have a Christmas Babe that brings light, and joy, and summer that never fades ~ the Christ-Child. He loves us too, for he once said that the most beautiful garments of man were not so lovely as those that come to us who neither toil nor spin."

The story was ended, and Lovie was filled with strange new thoughts, as she took her father's hand and said, "**Everything knows**, doesn't it Papa-Jack? Everything has its good time, but who'd ever thought about the **alive** down, away down in the ground, being so glad about the sun's turning around to come back."

Then Lovie had to talk about the wonderful teentsie-weentsie Baby Spring away down there, and how the wise old trees had found it first just like the Wise Men did the Baby-Christ. It was a rare Christmas talk Papa-Jack and his little girl had out in the white woods, and as they walked on they found the little stream fast asleep, tucked away under blankets of soft white. A rabbit came hopping by making funny little tracks in the snow. Lovie stopped and interviewed Sir Bunny and promised him and his family a royal Christmas dinner of parsnips and carrots. All at once her attention was called to

the great snowflakes which were spreading in wonderful shapes over her coat. "Oh, Papa-Jack, see, see," cried the child delightedly. "They are sky-flowers. Look, there's a daisy, and a star lily," and baring her pink palm, she held it out to catch them.

"But they won't stay in my hand, Papa. I want them to wait and let me look at them, Why won't they?"

"Because," answered the father, "the little frost-fairies of the sky-flowers as you call them cannot stand the warmth of your hand, and so vanish. But see what they have left behind."

"I don't see anything only my hands are wet," answered Lovie.

"That's it, dear, water."

"Why!" exclaimed the astonished child, "is it only water? All these beautiful flowers only water?"

"Don't you know dear," answered Papa-Jack, "how necessary it is for your summer blossoms to have water? Well, it is quite as much so for these winter blossoms, for without it there would be no snowflakes or ice or frost."

Then followed a delightful talk about the wonderful things water can do.

"Just to think, Papa-Jack, it is so delicious when one is thirsty, and so perfectly necessary when one is dirty, and the flowers and everything are partly made of it. And then it can jump on a sunbeam and ride up to the sky and be clouds or snow or gold dust at sunset. Oh, my, how wonderful everything is when you know about it."

The good father reminded his enthusiastic little girl that the folks at the bungalow would be looking for them. Aunt Joy and Grace and all the Day family were expected for Christmas.

We have just time for the least little hint of what Lovie did for Christmas. To Lovie the Christmas myth of Santa Claus stood for the great Love that never forgets anybody in its reckoning, and so, aided by her fadder-grand, and all her numerous friends, she sent the three boys out fixed up like Santa Clauses with gay sleds and jingling bells to dispense all kinds of toys and goodies and bounties to the "dear children" who had been at her birthday party. The Spirit of Christmas wrapped the great city, and selfishness and greed were forgotten in the joy of giving.

EPILOGUE:

My heart felt heavy that day in the Heritage Room, which is the archive library at Unity Village, when I realized that Myrtle Fillmore hadn't actually finished this charming, powerful story. Oh how I wanted to find its completion in the next issue of *Wee Wisdom*. Many hours were spent trying to discover it and then, to my ecstatic joy, there it was. No, by golly, it wasn't the completion after all. The entire thirteen chapters had just been reprinted. After experiencing disappointment, and also through that search seeing the evolution of *Wee Wisdom*, I found the answer. Myrtle Fillmore's healing ministry had grown to the place where she no longer even edited *Wee Wisdom*. The story would remain unfinished, because her time had been dedicated to the healing letters, prayer meetings, and the actual work of healing people. Again I saw this consciousness of service so clearly, and my respect for the co-founder deepened. She wasn't just talking about God, she truly experienced God and was dedicated to sharing God's promises of healing with others.

The story's essence needs no completion because it calls each of us to be about LIVING the principles of oneness, unity, and love. In Truth, the mystical message of "Lovie" has no ending. As we read and re-read this book, we can each incorporate into our lives the underlying principles, and from that perspective, live out the Reality of its message. Myrtle Fillmore's consciousness will continue to bless this planet through the expression of our lives.

— Rev. Lei Lanni Burt

STUDY QUESTIONS

From
"THE HIDDEN TREASURES
OF MYRTLE FILLMORE"
A Workshop Developed
by Rev. Lei Lanni Burt

1. Myrtle has an interesting writing style. What feeling does it create in you?

2. How does her writing style move you from the intellect into the heart?

3. What principles of metaphysics does Myrtle teach in this story?

4. What divine ideas do you find illustrated in these pages?

5. What is Myrtle's concept of love? (Chapter VII)

6. Share one personal insight you have gained from the story thus far, and write it down. How will you *live* this insight?

7. How does Myrtle describe the essence of life? (Chapter VIII)

8. Myrtle's concept of creation is told in the story form in Chapter IX. How would you write your own creation story?

9. Review pages 48-50. What attitude does Myrtle express about conditions or circumstances that we've named "evil" or "bad"?

10. Reflecting now on your own life — QUIETLY — can you apply your insight to something specific?

11. Myrtle loved the Scriptures, and this can be seen in the following passages. What parallels do you seen in:
    - John 13:34, Matthew 18:1-6,
        Matthew 5:14-16 and page 66-67
    - Matthew 11:15 and page 72-73
    - 1 Kings 19:11-12, Matthew 6:25-34
        and page 72-73

12. As Myrtle developed her story, what aspects of child-likeness did she address?

13. How do you relate and respond to her message:

> To enjoy without possession.
> To see without coveting.
> To have without holding.
> To be without seeming.
>
> In short, to be myself,
> Without desiring.
> Knowing all this is for me,
> For my pleasure and the
> Satisfaction of my immortal soul.
>
> To say "That I am monarch
> Of all I survey. My right
> Here is none to dispute."
>
> To be generous-hearted.
> What I see, others may see.
> What I enjoy, others may
> share also on equal terms with me.

Myrtle's Credo: found in her own handwriting after she died in 1931 (*Mother of Unity*, pg 171)

14. How does the Story of Lovie reflect or relate to Myrtle's credo?

15. Is there one idea, precept, or insight that you can apply to your life, right now, as a result of having experienced this story? If so, explain.

ABOUT
REV. LEI LANNI BURT

Rev. Lei Lanni Burt graduated from the Ministerial Education Program at Unity Village in 1988. During ministerial school, Lei Lanni had a vision to invite and empower congregants into spiritual maturity. Following graduation, she pioneered her first ministry in Nevada. It was while serving as Senior Minister in Santa Rosa, California that Lei Lanni was able to realize her vision as she developed and implemented her first Unity Chaplain Program. She brought this program with her to Unity of Phoenix in Arizona where she currently serves as Pastoral Care Minister and has been training Unity Chaplains since 1998. In 1999, she created a Trainers Workshop, opening the space for the Unity Chaplain Program to be brought to other ministries.

Lei Lanni has long served the Unity Community. Prior to entering Ministerial School, she held various positions in Unity ministries. She was a Licensed Unity Teacher and Spiritual Counselor. And, from 1994 to 2001 she was on the Licensing & Ordination Team of the Association of Unity Churches, providing leadership to the team as Chairperson for three years. Most recently Lei Lanni has been elected to serve at the Association of Unity Churches as a member on the Board of Trustees.

ABOUT THE ARTIST

Unity has had a major influence on Carole Fogle's life. Many of her ancestors were followers of Myrtle Fillmore, including Clara Palmer, a Unity author, early member of Silent Unity, and contributing editor to *Weekly Unity* magazine.

During the past fifteen years, Carole's chosen method of expression has been pen and ink drawings. She feels this affinity was greatly enhanced by her many years of exposure to the illustrations in the Unity publications, *Weekly Unity* and *Wee Wisdom.* "Being asked to illustrate **Lovie** is the greatest honor I have received as a member of the Unity community," states Carole, who became a Licensed Unity Teacher in 1995.